The Berenstain Bears®

REAP THE HARVEST

... Imitate those who through faith and patience inherit what has been promised.

—Hebrews 6:12

by Stan and Jan Berenstain
with Mike Berenstain

ZONDER**kidz**

Living
Lights™

Beginning Reader

It was summertime. School was closed for the year. Brother and Sister Bear were walking down a dusty road. They were thinking about how they should spend their summer vacation.

"We could just play," said Sister.

"Playing is fine," said
Brother. "But playing all the
time would be boring."

"We could go swimming," said Sister.

"Swimming is fine," said Brother.
"But we can't go swimming every day."

"We could go to the library," said Sister.

"Yes," said Brother. "Mama takes us to the library every Saturday. But what will we do the rest of the week?"

"Maybe we could get a job!" said Sister. "Papa says according to Proverbs, 'All hard work brings a profit.' Maybe we can make some money."

"That's a good idea," said Brother. "But what kind of job could we get? We're just cubs."

That's when they saw the sign. It was
hanging on Farmer Ben's front gate. It said:
HELP WANTED. SEE FARMER BEN.

"Well, yes," said Farmer Ben. "I do need help. But I was thinking of someone older. What could you cubs do to help?"

"All kinds of things," said the cubs.

"We could sweep the barn,

feed the chickens,

collect the eggs,

"Hmmm," said Farmer Ben. He thought for a while. Then he said, "All right. The job is yours. Here are some brooms. You can start by sweeping the barn."

"There's just one thing," said Sister. "If this is a job, we should get paid."

"Yes," said Brother. "How much will you pay us?"

"Hmmm," said Ben. "See that field? That's my cornfield, and corn is my cash crop."

"What's a cash crop?" asked Sister.

"A cash crop is what a farmer grows to make money," said Brother.

"I'll tell you what," said Ben. He took a piece of string and some sticks and marked off a corner of the field.

"If you do a good job, I'll pay you the money I get for all the corn that grows in that corner of the field."

"How much will that be?" asked Sister.

"Depends," said Farmer Ben.

"Depends on what?" asked Brother.

"Depends on how much rain
the Good Lord sends our way,"
said Ben. "Not too little; not too
much. Depends on cornbugs. In
a bad year, cornbugs can ruin a
crop. Depends on keeping the
crows from eating the seed—

that's why I'm making this scarecrow."

"So we won't know how much money we'll earn until the end of the summer," said Sister.

"No more than I will," said Farmer Ben. "That's the way it is with farming. Same way it is with faith ... our true reward comes later on—in God's good time."

So the cubs went to work.

They swept the barn.

They fed
the chickens.

They collected the eggs.

They slopped the hogs.

They called the cows.

HERE BOSSIE

They made sure the bull pen
was locked tight.

And they kept a close watch on their corner of the cornfield!

Brother watched the sky for rain.

Sister had bad dreams about cornbugs.

And when the crows were no longer afraid of Farmer Ben's scarecrow, Brother and Sister made a scarier one. It even scared Farmer Ben.

Working on the farm was hard, but it was fun too.

Brother and Sister both loved and respected all of God's creatures. And they made friends with the animals—

the chickens,

the pigs,

the cows.

Even Ben's big bull seemed
to like Brother and Sister.

But the best thing was having their own corner of the cornfield. The corn grew straight and tall and healthy.

"Farmer Ben told me the book of Timothy says, 'The hardworking farmer should be the first to receive a share of the crops,'" quoted Brother.

"Yessir," said Ben as he
got ready to harvest the corn.
"This is the finest cash crop
I've grown in years. You cubs
are going to do all right."

And they did. Their corner of the cornfield earned them many, many dollars. The farm had been blessed with a fine harvest indeed.

"Well," said Farmer Ben as he paid the cubs, "you should be proud of the good job you did all summer. Now don't spend it all in one place."

"We won't," said Brother. "But we will *put* it all in one place—the bank!"

"That's right," said Sister. "It took us a long time to earn this money. We want to keep it at least as long as it took to earn it."

The Berenstain Bears'
PERFECT
FISHING
SPOT

She speaks with wisdom,

and faithful instruction is on her tongue.

She watches over the affairs of her household ...

—Proverbs 31:26–27

by Stan and Jan Berenstain
with Mike Berenstain

 ZONDER**kidz**

Living
Lights™

Beginning Reader

Do you know what I wish?
I wish that for dinner
we could have fish.

A fine, fat fish, tender and sweet.
There is nothing better
in the world to eat!
Thanks be to God
for that delicious treat!

A fish would be fine.
But there's no need to fuss.
Just go and buy one
from Grizzly Gus.

May Sister and I come with you, Dad?

Yes, indeed.
Of course, my lad.
Spending time with you two
makes my heart glad!

But, Papa!
Ma said go to Grizzly Gus!

That's true, my son.
But just between us,
if you want a fish
that's tender and sweet,
a fish that's a wonderful treat
for a bear to eat—

then dig up some worms,
get out your pole,

GRIZZLY
FISH

and head for your favorite
fishing hole.

Your fishing hole
looks small, Papa Bear.
Can there really be
a big fish in there?

Of course there can.
I've got one now!
Just watch your dad.
He'll show you how
to catch a fish
that's tender and sweet,
a fish that's a treat
for a bear to eat!

Papa, that fish
may be tender and sweet,
but it's much too small
for us to eat.

Hmm. The big ones have all
been caught, you see,
caught years ago
by guess who? ME!

I know a better
fishing spot!

I can taste that fish,
tender, hot,
a fish to do
our family proud...

But Pa, it says
NO FISHING ALLOWED!

But who will know
if I drop my hook?

He will, Pa!
The fish warden! Look!

NO FISHING

FISH
WARDEN

I see, I see.
Good day to you!
Er…my cubs and I
were enjoying the view!
So sorry! God bless!
Such a good job you do!

This fish, Dad,
will you catch it soon?
I think it must be
after noon!

Don't bother me
with questions, please.
I know a spot
just past those trees!

Hook and worm,
now do your duty
in this place of God's
most peaceful beauty.

Look, cubs! Look!
I've got a bite!
Whatever I've hooked,
just look at it fight!

Look how it thrashes!
Look how it sloshes!

Dad, that isn't a fish!
It's a pair of galoshes!

This way, cubs!
Follow me!
We will get our fish
from the deep blue sea!
God provides, he'll make sure
we have what we need!

BOATS
RENTED

Look at them all!
They'll sink our boat!
Throw'em back!
We must stay afloat!

Help! Help!
Look, Papa Bear!
We're going up!
Up in the air!

Boat and all!
In a great big net!
We're in the air
and very wet!

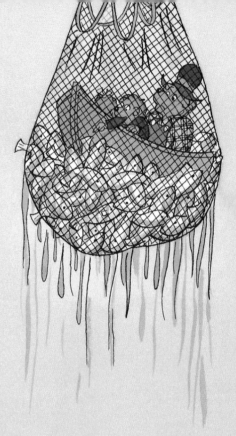

We're coming down
on a great big boat—
the biggest
fishing boat afloat!

You got caught with our fish.
Sorry about that!
Excuse me, sir—
but that's one of ours
under your hat!

Pa, we still have
a fish to get!
We have not caught
our dinner yet!

No problem, son.
No need to fuss!
We'll buy our fish
from Grizzly Gus!

BUY OUR FISH
FROM GRIZZLY GUS?

My best advice
to both of you
is to do what Mama
says to do!

God's blessed Gus with
the perfect fishing spot.
We never really
had a shot.

Ah! A fish that's tender.
A fish that's sweet.
A fish that's good
for a bear family to eat!
God bless this food.
God bless this treat!

The Berenstain Bears®
The Trouble with Secrets

*"Dear friends, let us love one another,
for love comes from God."*

—1 John 4:7

by Stan and Jan Berenstain
with Mike Berenstain

ZONDERkidz

Living Lights™

Beginning Reader

There go Brother and Sister Bear.
Friends Lizzy and Fred
want to know where.

Lizzy and Fred want to know why
their friends have that
secret look in their eye.

Is this something our friends would do?
Keep a secret from me and you?

Where are our friends going today?
We know what!
We'll ask Mr. Jay!

But he just says, "Screech!"
He will not say
where Brother and Sister
are going today.

He must have promised
he would not say!

So we follow our friends
to where the path bends.

We follow and follow
and follow along.
We hear Mrs. Cricket singing her song
of how thankful she is
that God's love is so strong.

We ask Mrs. Cricket
if she will say
where Brother and Sister
are going today.

But she just chirps.
She will not say.
She will not give the secret away.
She must have promised
she would not say!

We make sure we are not seen
as we move through the forest
so dark and so green.

We follow and follow
and follow along.
Friends Brother and Sister
are still going strong.

Should we ask Mr. Skunk?
He might know
where Brother and Sister
are about to go.

Hmmm. On second thought ...
we don't think we ought!

We follow our friends
through Great Grizzly Bog,
where Mrs. Frog suns herself
on Great Hollow Log ...

and ribbits a prayer
of thanks and praise
for flies and water and hot, sunny days.

Should we ask Mrs. Frog?
It's worth a try.

But she sticks out her tongue
and catches a fly.
Yuck! We think it's time to say good-bye.

So we follow and follow
and follow along.

Friends Brother and Sister
are still going strong.

Now we see
old Mr. Croc

sound asleep
on a big rock.

We do not bother
old Mr. Croc.
We leave him sleeping
on his rock.

We're getting tired following along
and following and following
and following along.
There is no need for secrets or sneaking.
God made us friends!
If they'd share, we'd stop peeking!

Will this following
NEVER END?

But wait! Brother and Sister
are rounding a bend!

And look at that! Standing right there!
The secret of Brother
and Sister Bear!
It's a clubhouse they made
from pieces of junk.

"Who told?" asked Brother.
"Was it Mr. Skunk?
Or Frog or Croc or Cricket or Jay
who told you our secret
and showed you the way?"

"Nobody told.
Though you were really going strong,
we just followed and followed
and followed along!"
Brother and Sister looked glum for a while.
But being upset
just isn't their style!
Then they both began to smile.

They were glad God blessed them
with friends like Lizzy and Fred.
"We're glad you followed us here," they said.

"Secrets are fun.
But it's more fun to share!
So welcome!" said Brother
and Sister Bear.